W9-CRS-713

What's the Matter, Sylvie, Can't You Ride?

What's the Matter, Sylvie,

Story and pictures by

Can't You Ride?

KAREN BORN ANDERSEN

The Dial Press / New York

Published by The Dial Press
1 Dag Hammarskjold Plaza
New York, New York 10017

Copyright © 1981 by Karen Born Andersen
All rights reserved. Manufactured in the U.S.A.
First printing
Design by Denise Cronin Neary

Library of Congress Cataloging in Publication Data

Andersen, Karen Born.
What's the matter, Sylvie, can't you ride?

Summary: Sylvie experiences the trials and tribulations
of learning to ride her two-wheel bicycle.
[1. Bicycles and bicycling—Fiction]   I. Title.
PZ7.A51899Wh   [E]   80-12514
ISBN 0-8037-9607-2
ISBN 0-8037-9621-8 (lib bdg.)

The art for each picture consists of an ink
and wash drawing with two color overlays,
all reproduced as halftone.

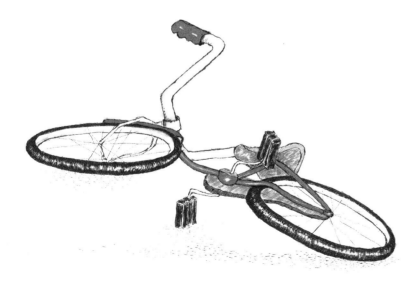

For my mother and father

Early in the morning Sylvie climbed on her bike once more. She sat on the seat for a long time, with her feet touching the ground. She wondered if she would ever make it down the hill that went by George's house.

She pushed a little to get the bike going, then she jerked her feet up to the pedals. But her feet wouldn't stay. They wanted to be back safe on the sidewalk, and there was nothing she could do about it.

She pushed harder, and the bike started rolling, but it wobbled from side to side. She got scared and couldn't breathe, and her feet shot down to save her.

So she sat again, looking down the block.

In the afternoon Sylvie's mother rode up on her bike. "Let's ride," she said.

"But I can't," said Sylvie, whining a little.

"It's easy. Come on and try. We'll ride together."

"BUT I CAN'T!" screamed Sylvie.

"Okay. Do whatever you want," said her mother as she rode past, fast.

Sylvie walked her bike a little while, and then sat on the seat with her feet on the ground.

Virginia rode by. "Can't you ride?" she yelled. "I learned *last* year."

Sylvie tried to concentrate on her mother speeding toward her.
Virginia rode by again. "What's the matter? Can't you ride?"

Sylvie didn't answer, but her mother said, "She can—she's just practicing."

"That's all I need," Sylvie thought. "Now she knows my mother's a liar."

The next morning Sylvie's father came out to watch when she sat on her bike.

"Let me see your progress," he said.

She pushed off and coasted awhile, with her feet jerking up and down from the pedals to the sidewalk.

"Hey, that's just great!" yelled her father. "Great, Sylvie, great."

She walked her bike to the end of the block so she wouldn't have to hear him anymore.

When she turned around, he'd gone back inside.

The next week Sylvie pushed her bike to the basketball court before anybody was up. "Maybe I can ride if nobody's watching," she thought.

But she couldn't. Her feet still wouldn't stay on the pedals, and she got sick of the short, jarring movements. She hated the way she got so scared. Nobody else was scared. Nobody else thought they would splat all bloody on the cement, and they all went a hundred times faster than she did.

She kicked her bike so hard, her toe hurt through her boots. As she limped furiously home she saw George. He said "Hi," but all Sylvie said was "I hope it rots in the rain."

That night Sylvie's toe ached so much that she couldn't sleep, and
she cried because her birthday bike was lost and probably ruined.

It wasn't, though, when she went back for it in the morning.

She pushed off again and fought to keep her feet on the pedals. But they didn't seem to be *her* feet, and they just kept jerking downward.

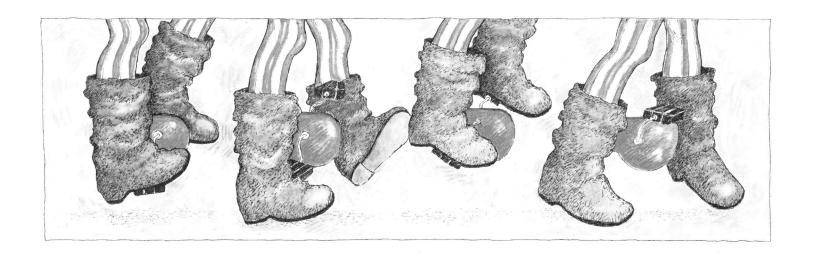

"All right, that's it. Who wants to ride anyway?" Sylvie said over and over as she sat on the seat, pushing fast with her feet, going home.

Virginia whizzed by, and Sylvie pushed harder, faster.

She'd go home and get a hammer and smash up the bike. Leave the pieces for the garbage man!

She was so mad, she didn't notice that her feet were speeding up on the sidewalk. And she didn't notice that she had started down the hill she had always avoided.

By the time Sylvie realized how fast she was going, she was too angry to care.

"So what if I crash? So what if I break my head? So what if I wreck this stupid bike?"

She put her feet on the pedals and held on.

Down she roared, and the bike didn't wobble. It didn't seem about to fall over. It felt smooth and steady and perfectly safe.

"Hey, this is it!" she yelled. "I can do it!"

It was terrific to be speeding along, surely, swiftly, with no fear at all.

When she got to the end of the hill, Sylvie started pedaling. The bike *still* didn't wobble.

She saw George sitting on his bike, with his feet on the ground, watching her sadly.

"CAN'T YOU RIDE?" yelled Sylvie as she sailed past.